Laura's Star

Friends Forever

KLAUS BAUMGART lives with his family in Berlin. The LAURA'S STAR series has had multi-million sales worldwide. It has been broadcast on TV throughout Europe, including in the UK, and the first title, LAURA'S STAR, has been made into a film. Klaus Baumgart was the first German author/illustrator to be shortlisted for the Children's Book Award in 1999 for LAURA'S STAR.

Also available by Klaus Baumgart:

Picture Books

LAURA'S STAR

LAURA'S SECRET

First Readers

LAURA'S STAR AND THE NEW TEACHER

LAURA'S STAR AND THE SEARCH FOR SANTA

LAURA'S STAR AND THE SPECIAL PONY

Activity Book

LAURA'S STAR STICKER ACTIVITY BOOK

LITTLE TIGER PRESS
An imprint of Magi Publications
1 The Coda Centre, 189 Munster Road, London SW6 6AW
www.littletigerpress.com

First published in Great Britain 2010
Originally published in Germany 2008
by Baumhaus Verlag, Frankfurt

Translation by Katharina Kwasniowski

A CIP catalogue record for this book is available from the British Library

HBK – ISBN: 978-1-84895-104-4 • PBK – ISBN: 978-1-84895-112-9
Printed in China • LTP/1800/0103/0610

2 4 6 8 10 9 7 5 3 1

Laura's Star

Friends Forever

Klaus Baumgart

English text by Fiona Waters

LITTLE TIGER PRESS
London

The Friendship Tree

"Look Sophie, there's a new leaf on our tree!" Laura called excitedly.

Sophie ran over to the rose bed and knelt down beside her. Together they had planted a chestnut in the autumn in amongst the roses, and now the first tiny leaves were showing. Laura patted the earth down around the little tree and

Sophie watered it very carefully.

Laura closed her eyes and imagined how exciting it would be to climb to the very top of the tree when it was fully grown. She and

Sophie would be up there alone, sitting on a branch in a great, green cave, with their legs dangling, and talking, while all around them the leaves rustled.

"This will be our secret," promised Laura. "Our very own friendship tree!"

"Ooh yes," whispered Sophie. "It's so exciting!"

Sophie was Laura's best friend, and they did everything together. Now they would both look after the tiny tree as well!

Laura did also have another very special friend, her star. Every night, when she looked out of her window, her star would be there in the sky, twinkling down at her. The star had helped Laura many times before and was her other best friend.

As Laura and Sophie walked indoors, Sophie said, "I can't wait until Monday!"

"I know," smiled Laura. "It's your birthday! Shall we make paper chains and lanterns to decorate your flat?"

They collected paper and scissors and went back out into the garden. They spread the brightly-coloured paper out on the bench. Laura began folding tiny paper butterflies, which she was going to glue to straws.

"Oh bother! I've forgotten the glue," she said.

"I'll go and get it," said Sophie, and she ran away across the yard, leaving Laura on the bench.

Laura held up two colourful butterflies in her hands. "The blue one is for Sophie, and the red one is for me!" she thought.

Very gently, Laura made the butterflies fly up in the air, and as she did she thought how butterflies just like these would fly through the branches of their little chestnut tree.

She tiptoed across to the small tree and laid the butterflies on the tiny leaves. The wind made their wings flutter.

While Laura was looking at the tree, her little brother, Tommy, came running out of the flat. He had a ball in his hand.

"Come on, Laura," he shouted, "let's play a game!"

But Laura shook her head. "I'm too busy just now," she answered.

"Oh, please, Laura, please," begged Tommy. "Look, I can play really well now," and he threw the ball up in the air and kicked it hard. The ball went up and up. "Yippee!" yelled Tommy. "Almost up to the second floor!"

But Laura was watching the ball nervously as it started to fall, straight towards the rose bed!

"Oh no!" shrieked Tommy. He rushed up to catch the ball, and Laura held up her hands too. But they both missed. It landed with a thump, right in the middle of the roses!

"Phew!" breathed Tommy. "It hasn't damaged any of the

roses," and he bent over to pick up the ball.

But Laura stood there, frozen stiff. Tommy's ball had not hit any of the roses, but it had landed right

on top of the chestnut tree! The tiny plant lay crumpled on the ground, the paper butterflies lying beside it, all covered in earth.

"Our friendship tree!" Laura cried. Horrified, Tommy realised what had happened. He tried to straighten up the tree, but it was no good. The delicate stem was broken.

"Oh, Laura, I am so s-sorry!" stammered Tommy. "I didn't mean for that to happen."

"Saying sorry doesn't save the poor tree," cried Laura desperately. She was really sad and really cross with Tommy all at the same time. "Whatever is Sophie going to say?" she sighed.

Tommy looked really worried. "Don't tell her," he begged. "Please, Laura, don't tell her! She won't ever let me play with you both again."

"But it's your fault," Laura answered crossly, and Tommy began to cry. He bent down and picked up the paper butterflies and tried to wipe the soil off them.

"Oh, leave them alone, it's too late to save them," said Laura and, snatching them from Tommy, she crumpled them up in her hand.

But when she looked at him she suddenly felt very sorry for him. He looked so miserable. It really wasn't his fault that the ball had hit the little tree.

"Do stop crying, Tommy," she said gently. "I won't tell Sophie, I promise."

"You promise?" sobbed Tommy.

"I promise," said Laura. "But you'd better go back inside again before she sees you."

Tommy nodded and, picking up his ball, he ran quickly into the flat.

A Big Argument

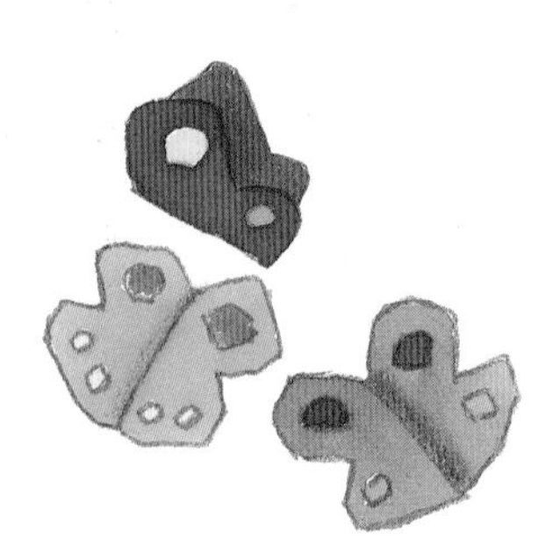

When Sophie returned with the glue, Laura was sitting on the bench again. She had tried to make two new butterflies but they were not nearly as beautiful as the first two.

As well as the glue, Sophie had a cup of water in her hand.

"This is for our friendship tree!"

she smiled and turned to walk over to the rose bed.

Laura stood up immediately – how was she going to stop Sophie from discovering what had happened to their tree?

"I, I don't think our tree will be thirsty yet," she gasped. "My grandfather says we shouldn't water plants too much."

But Sophie had already reached the rose bed. She stood looking at the broken tree in dismay.

"Laura, whatever has happened to our tree?" she cried.

"I don't . . . well, I have no idea," stuttered Laura.

Sophie looked at her with a frown. "But you were here all the time. You must have seen what happened," she said.

Laura felt herself blushing. "Yes, I was of course, but . . . I mean. No. Well, I was gone for a moment, I went to the bathroom," she tried to explain.

Sophie frowned even harder.

"Laura, I think you're telling fibs," she said crossly.

Laura shook her head and said quickly, "I'm not!" but she felt her face getting even redder. She was upset that she had not thought about how she was going to tell Sophie what had happened.

"But you *are* telling me fibs!" shouted Sophie. "I know you are."

"I am not!" Laura shouted back in desperation, her face bright red.

"Then tell me, just how has our tree been broken? Who did it?" Sophie demanded.

Laura didn't reply. What could she do? She had promised Tommy she would not tell on him.

"Great!" Sophie muttered. "Don't tell me then. But if you are not telling me the truth then you are no longer my best friend!"

With that, Sophie emptied the water over the roses, then packed up her things and walked away silently.

* * *

Laura felt utterly miserable. She couldn't eat anything at suppertime and then later, when she went to bed, she could not get to sleep. She tossed and turned and eventually got up to look out of her window.

Up in the sky, one star was

especially bright. It was her star who had been her friend for so long.

The star tumbled down towards Laura, sparkling as it fell.

"Oh Star," she sighed, and then she told the star everything that had happened that day. "What can I do? If I tell Sophie that Tommy broke our tree she will never play with him again. Besides, I did promise him I wouldn't tell. But if I don't tell Sophie, she will never be my friend again."

The star shone brightly and Laura felt a bit better already in its friendly glow.

"However am I going to make it up with Sophie again?" she said. "I'm not sure that she will forgive me tomorrow. She's such a special friend."

As Laura climbed back into bed and snuggled down again, she whispered, "I am so glad you are there. Thank you, Star," and as she finally fell asleep, the star twirled back up into the sky.

A Present from Tommy

But the next day, everything seemed to be even worse. At school, Sophie didn't speak to Laura at all. They both sat side by side, staring ahead and not looking at each other.

Laura decided that she would try to talk to Sophie during break. As soon as the bell rang, she ran to the shop and bought two drinks, one for

herself and one for Sophie. But as she walked up to her, Laura saw Sophie laughing and chatting to Paula. "Is Paula her new best friend?" Laura wondered sadly as she stood there with a drink in each hand.

Suddenly Laura was not at all thirsty. She didn't know what to do. Should she try to talk to Sophie after school, when they walked home together? But that didn't work out either because after school Sophie didn't wait for Laura as usual but quickly packed her bag and was out of the door before Laura could say anything to her. Laura was sure that from now on Sophie was going to walk home with Paula.

Head down, Laura sadly set off for home all alone.

Tommy opened the front door for her. “Daddy is making pancakes!” he shouted happily. But when he saw Laura’s unhappy face he asked anxiously, “Is there something wrong?”

Laura nodded and suddenly a tear ran down her cheek.

"Sophie won't be my friend anymore because I lied to her yesterday about the friendship tree," she answered sadly.

Tommy gulped but said nothing.

Laura went into her bedroom and, flinging herself down on to her bed, pulled a blanket over her head. What on earth was she going to do? It was the weekend now but soon it would be Monday. And Monday was Sophie's birthday! Laura just couldn't imagine a worse day.

And then she remembered the present she had bought for Sophie. She leant over the side of the bed and

pulled it out from underneath where she had hidden it. It was a small, green watering can, and it had been meant for watering the friendship tree. But what would Sophie do with it now?

Laura pushed the watering can

back right into the furthest corner under the bed. Sophie was not going to want any presents from Laura now. And she burst into tears again and sobbed into her pillow.

After a while, there was a gentle knock at the door and Tommy came in quietly.

"Look, Laura," he said, and he pressed something into her hand. It was small and round, and when she opened her eyes there was a chestnut lying in her hand.

"I kept it last autumn," Tommy explained. "We could plant it and a new tree would grow, and we could give it to Sophie. Then she wouldn't be cross anymore!"

Laura looked at the chestnut. It was old and very wrinkled. Could anything grow out of it?

"Thank you, Tommy," Laura sniffed. "We can try," she said softly.

Next morning, Laura and Tommy found a flowerpot and filled it with earth. They pressed the chestnut deep into the soil and watered it – not too much, just as Grandfather had said. Then they put the pot in a sunny spot on the window sill.

Laura looked at the pot anxiously. It had taken the friendship tree months to sprout. Would it grow faster in the warmth of the flat, in time for Monday? Laura was fidgety with worry.

An Anxious Weekend

For the whole of the rest of Saturday and all of Sunday, Tommy and Laura kept a very close watch on the flowerpot. Every half hour they gave it a tiny drop of water to keep it moist. Laura even played her flute to the chestnut because Grandfather had once told her that plants grow better with music.

But absolutely nothing happened.

On Sunday afternoon, Mum was playing at a concert. Tommy was sitting with Dad, who was reading out loud to him. But Laura simply could not sit still for a moment. She wandered about the flat, returning every moment to look at the flowerpot. But there was absolutely no sign of a sprout.

As she glanced out of the window, she saw Sophie down below.

Laura dashed to the balcony and was going to call after her when she saw that Sophie was not alone. Paula was with her. Her new best friend, thought Laura sadly. Laura had never felt more lonely as she watched her best friend walk away down the street with someone new. "That should be me," whispered Laura and her eyes filled with tears.

* * *

It was getting dark and the first stars were appearing in the sky. Laura's special star was shining above the house as she stood on the balcony.

"Oh Star, what do you think I should do? Should I just stop

thinking about Sophie?" Laura asked anxiously.

The star floated closer and sent showers of sparkling light over Laura.

"Can you help me, Star? I so want to make up with Sophie but I have no idea how I can do that now," she sighed.

The star drifted down towards Laura, tapped her gently on the shoulder, and darted into the house through the balcony door. It glided along the passage and then hovered over the telephone.

Laura shook her head. "I couldn't possibly call her," she said firmly. "As soon as she hears my voice she will hang up immediately!"

The star twirled for a moment as though it was thinking and then whizzed into Laura's bedroom. Laura followed the star in and watched as it circled round her desk. Then it slipped into one of the drawers.

Laura wondered what on earth the star was up to. And then an envelope slid from the drawer and fluttered to the ground.

"You think I should write a letter to Sophie?" Laura asked as the star whizzed out of the drawer and sparkled round the room again.

"Whatever can I say?" she thought.

Then her special star twirled down and touched Laura softly on the shoulder.

"Well, I can only try, Star," and she sat down at her desk, chose some pretty writing paper and picked up her pen. After a few moments, she began to write.

DEAR SOPHIE,
I AM REALLY VERY SORRY.
I DIDN'T WANT TO LIE TO YOU
BUT I HAD PROMISED NOT TO TELL
ON THE PERSON WHO BROKE OUR
FRIENDSHIP TREE. IT WAS AN
ACCIDENT. PLEASE CAN WE BE
FRIENDS AGAIN?
LOVE,
LAURA

Laura folded the letter and put it in the envelope the star had taken out of the drawer.

For Sophie she wrote on it.

"Right," she said, "that's done."

And Laura felt much happier. Now she just had to give the letter to Sophie. But she was still a bit scared. Would Sophie ever want to be her friend again?

The Magic of the Star

With the letter in her hand, the flowerpot firmly under her arm and her special star still hovering by her side, Laura walked to Sophie's flat. When she was standing at the front door, she didn't know if she was brave enough to ring the bell and give the letter to Sophie. What if Sophie closed the door right in her face? She laid the letter on the doorstep and put the flowerpot beside it. She looked at it sadly once more. "Will it ever grow?" she whispered.

But just then the star floated up to the flowerpot and floated round it, stardust trickling on to the soil. Then the star bent forward and lightly touched the pot. And suddenly Laura realised that she had been mistaken: the chestnut was sprouting! There was a tiny shoot just peeping out of the earth.

And with a sigh of relief, Laura realised that everything might be all right after all.

"Now, Star, we have to be very quick," she said. She took a deep breath and put her finger firmly on the bell. Then she darted down the stairs, the star following closely after her, and hid round the corner. No sooner had she reached her hiding place than the door opened and Sophie stuck her head out and looked all around.

Sophie didn't see Laura, but she spotted the letter and the flowerpot on the doorstep. She picked up the envelope, opened it and began to read Laura's letter. Then she looked

at the flowerpot, and Laura could see that she was smiling. Laura took a step forward in her excitement and the step creaked.

Sophie looked up from the flowerpot. "Is that you, Laura?" she asked happily.

Laura hardly dared look at Sophie, but she came out from her hiding place, blushing in embarrassment. Sophie looked down again at the flowerpot.

"Laura, is that a chestnut tree?" she asked shyly.

Laura nodded. "It's for you," she said quietly. "Please can this be our new friendship tree?"

"Oh Laura," Sophie cried happily, "of course it can! I am so sorry too. I know you must have had a good reason not to tell me who broke our first tree. I've wanted to talk to you ever since it happened but I thought you wouldn't want to be my friend after I was so mean to you."

Laura put her arms around Sophie. "Of course I want to be your friend! You are my *best* friend," Laura said with a huge grin.

"You'll be my best friend forever!"

"Great, now I can have my birthday party tomorrow after all," laughed Sophie.

"Were you going to cancel your party?" asked Laura.

Sophie nodded. "I couldn't have celebrated my birthday without my best friend. I've been looking forward to it for so long!" Sophie smiled. "I will see you tomorrow."

"Until tomorrow," promised Laura, and she skipped off down the stairs as happy as could be.

As she stepped outside, Laura could see her star, her special star, shining brightly in the sky. She waved at it.

"Oh Star, thank you so much. Sophie and I are best friends again," she smiled.

And the star twinkled back down at her.

Sophie's Birthday Party

"I really don't think I should come," said Tommy for the tenth time as Laura dragged him up the stairs to Sophie's flat.

"But Sophie invited you specially, Tommy! We are best of friends again, everything is fine," promised Laura.

"I still don't think I should be

here," repeated Tommy and he looked as if he had really bad toothache.

Laura rang the bell, and Sophie opened the door with a big smile on her face. "Come in!" she said. "You are the first to arrive."

Laura pushed Tommy and he hung his head in shame.

"Sophie, I have something I need to tell you," he muttered.

Puzzled, she asked, "What is it?"

Tommy took a deep breath. "It was me, Sophie. I broke your tree. I hit it with my ball, but it was an accident, honestly," he explained.

Sophie looked at him with a frown. But then she smiled. "Well, no wonder Laura wouldn't tell me who the culprit was. But it doesn't matter now because we have a lovely new tree which is even better than the first one. And it has grown since yesterday!"

Everything for the birthday party was laid out in the living room. The lanterns that Sophie and Laura had made were hanging from the ceiling, and Laura's butterflies were fastened round the straws. In pride of place on the window sill stood the flowerpot with the little chestnut tree.

They all looked at the flowerpot. Laura was amazed to see that the little tree seemed to have grown even more since she last saw it.

"It seems to be growing much faster than our first tree," thought Laura. "I wonder if my special star has really worked some magic?"

Sophie touched the soil with her fingertip. "I think I need to give it a drink again," she said to Laura, and turned to go into the kitchen to get a cup of water.

"Perhaps you should open your present first," smiled Laura, and she held out a parcel.

Sophie opened it excitedly. "Oh, it's a watering can!" she cried. "I can use it straight away," and when she had filled the watering can, she watered the chestnut very carefully.

Then more and more guests arrived. They played lots of games and ate delicious birthday cake. It was a splendid party, and when everyone else had gone, Laura, Sophie and Tommy went outside and planted the little friendship tree in a safe place in the garden.

Later that night, when Laura was tucked up in bed, she looked happily at the sky, and there was her special star, twinkling at her.

"Thank you so much, dear Star. Our new friendship tree is growing very fast and Sophie is my best friend again.

We'll be friends forever!" Laura snuggled down, a big smile on her face, as her special star twirled and sparkled high up in the sky.

Other Laura's Star First Readers to collect

LAURA'S STAR AND THE NEW TEACHER

It's the new school year and Laura is moving to a new class. She's really excited about it, until she hears that her new teacher is really strict. Suddenly Laura doesn't want to go back to school. Can her special friend, the star, help her find the courage to face Mrs Williamson?

LAURA'S STAR AND THE SPECIAL PONY

Laura longs to have a pony of her own. When she meets a little pony who needs a new home for the winter, Laura is determined to help. Then her friend, the star, gives her a wonderful idea . . .

LAURA'S STAR AND THE SEARCH FOR SANTA

Laura can't wait to go away for Christmas, but her little brother, Tommy, is worried that Santa won't be able to find them in their holiday cottage. Will Laura's special star help them out once more?